*This book is dedicated to my granddaughter Abbey,
who is a very sweet and special little girl.*

Hi, I'm Gary Richmond, and I'm a zoo keeper. As a zoo keeper, I've learned a lot about God's wonderful animals. At the same time, I've also learned a lot about God.

This true story is about a wolf named Niki who thought he was a dog. I think you'll like it.

In 1966 a young married couple answered a newspaper ad. It read, "Wolf pups for sale, $175. Call SY 56781." They had always wanted to own an unusual pet.

They went to see the wolf pups. The owner brought out three gray balls of fur. All of them were wagging their tails and whining happily. The little male wolf ran to the young couple and jumped up to be held. The wife snuggled him close to her cheek. The wolf pup licked her face and ear.

"We'll take this one!" she said.

"That wolf thinks he's a dog," said the man. "He's the friendliest wolf I've ever seen. His daddy is good with most folks. But there are a few he doesn't like. They have to watch out, or he'll get them good. That pup's different though, at least right now."

The couple wasn't listening very well. They were hugging and playing with this happy wolf puppy. The husband gave the man $175. Then they carried the excited puppy to their car.

The young couple was so thrilled. The wife held the pup on her lap. He slept most of the way home. On the way, they decided to name the little wolf Niki. They went by the market and spent the rest of their savings. They bought dog food, a red collar, dog toys and a bed for Niki.

Niki's two favorite things to do were digging and chewing. He chewed up everything in sight, even shoes and furniture. Niki was always digging up the backyard trying to make a den; as any wolf would normally do. By the time Niki was six months old, he weighed over 100 pounds. He was playful and loving to everyone.

One evening the young couple left Niki in the backyard digging away. The wife said, "We're going to the store. Be a good boy, Niki; we'll be back in a little while with a treat for you." Niki looked up. His soft gray eyes met their smiles with love. He looked a little silly with dirt on his nose. They laughed at him and left for the store.

Niki had dug a much larger hole than they had noticed. It led under the wooden fence into the neighbors' backyard. Niki soon squeezed under the fence and explored the yard. When Niki saw the neighbors' cat, he began chasing it. He chased the cat to the front yard and past several houses on the block. Finally the cat jumped into another backyard and got away.

Niki had never been out of the yard without his leash. He was lost. Suddenly he had feelings he had never known before. A wild, adult wolf may run 30 miles in a day looking for food without getting tired. So, Niki looked both directions. He decided to run toward the pretty, setting sun.

No one in the neighborhood saw Niki leave. Niki ran slowly through the city, at about eight miles an hour. Before long Niki had run 12 miles from home. But he wasn't tired. So, he just kept running all night long.

Back at home the young couple were very upset. They were driving the streets near their home looking for Niki. The young wife was crying like they had lost their child. Niki seemed to them like he was their child. But they never found him. They checked the local Humane Society (they take care of lost animals). No luck. The couple was very sad.

By the next morning, Niki was 30 miles from home. He was completely lost! He was getting hungry, so he began to look in backyards for dog food. It was 8:30 in the morning. A retired doctor saw Niki in his yard. He shut the gate trapping the wolf.

The old doctor called the Humane Society. They came and captured Niki. Niki was gentle. But the animal control officer took special care with him. The officer was not sure Niki was really a dog. Niki wore a collar and seemed very tame. Still, he looked like a wolf.

When they arrived at the Humane Society, several employees came to look at Niki. Some thought he was just a mix of shepherd dogs. Others said he was a husky breed. But a few agreed with the officer that Niki was a wolf. Niki had no dog tag on his collar. So, there was no one for the shelter to call. All they could do was keep Niki for 30 days and hope someone came to get him.

The young couple never dreamed Niki would run 30 miles away; so they never checked in San Marino. Niki's 30 days went by quickly. If someone didn't claim Niki, the Humane Society would have to destroy him.

Finally, Niki only had two days left. The Humane Society supervisor called the Los Angeles Zoo. He asked for a zoo keeper to come and tell them if Niki was a dog or a wolf. The zoo wanted a male wolf. So, they sent a senior zoo keeper right out to look at Niki.

The zoo keeper arrived at the Humane Society. It took the keeper just two seconds to say this: "Friends, you've found a wolf. The zoo will be happy to give him a good home." A cheer went up from the staff. They loved Niki and didn't want to see him hurt.

On the way back to the zoo, the senior keeper decided a tame wolf should have a name. He said to Niki, "You look like a Lobo to me. That's what I'm going to call you." The young wolf licked his hand as if to agree. From then on he was only called Lobo. Lobo is the Spanish word for wolf.

When they arrived at the zoo, the first thing Lobo
heard was a gentle whine. Then he saw Missy — a beautiful
lady wolf. She had soft gray eyes that smiled at everybody.
She was never mean. Lobo wondered if he was seeing a wolf
angel. He kept looking at the keeper. His eyes said, "Is this
my surprise? Is she really for me?"

It was love at first sight. Lobo pulled the keeper to his new cage where Missy stood waiting. First, they sniffed at each other. Then they began to play tag, wrestle, and race. When they were tired, Lobo laid down and Missy put her head on his neck. They were in wolf heaven. They would stay together as wolf mates for life.

Lobo also made another friend — his keeper, Al Bristacoff. Al played with Lobo every day. Lobo loved to be petted. He would lean against the wire of his cage so people could pet him.

It was almost a year later. Five strong, healthy wolf puppies were born to Missy and Lobo. Lobo was a good father and husband. He was careful not to step on the pups. They were always attacking his big legs and falling in front of him. When he laid down, they tugged on his ears. They pulled on the hair around his nose and bothered him. He was so proud of them.

Several weeks later, the zoo photographer, Gib Brush, came to take a wolf family picture. While Gib and his helpers set up their cameras, Lobo and Missy seemed upset. They paced back and forth. Often they ran to the gate to stare at the photographers and their equipment. None of the zoo keepers were really worried. Lobo and Missy had always been gentle and loving.

Finally, Gib was ready to take the picture. Al led the photographers into the wolf cage. The puppies were playing as usual. Lobo stood in front of the pups and stared at Gib. Al noticed that Lobo's hair was standing on end. So, he moved over to pet Lobo and calm him down.

Gib kept moving around trying to get a good angle for the photo. Lobo probably thought Gib was trying to hurt the pups.

Suddenly, Lobo exploded with a horrible growl and bark. He charged Gib angrily. He grabbed Gib's leg below the knee and clamped down with his huge jaws. Everyone was shocked when they heard Gib's leg crack. Al grabbed Lobo and pulled him off Gib. Quickly, Gib's helper pulled Gib out of the cage. Only then did Lobo calm down and lick Al's hand.

Gib was rushed to the local hospital. X-rays showed that his leg was badly broken. He would wear a cast for several months. Al knew that Lobo was no longer safe for everyone to pet. But he was still friendly to most people.

It was a pretty June morning. A young couple decided to take their 4-year-old child to the zoo. When they got to the wolf cage, the couple looked at each other sadly. It had been nearly five years since Niki had run away. But they still missed him.

Lobo and Missy were showing off their third litter of puppies. The whole wolf family was playing together. One wolf pup was hanging from Lobo's ear. The crowd laughed, and so did the couple.

Lobo had been ignoring the crowd. Suddenly one woman's laugh sounded familiar. He knew that voice. Something deep inside him stirred. Warm memories came back to him. He looked at the lady, and the man. Then he remembered car rides, being snuggled, chasing balls and digging in the yard.

Lobo began wagging his tail and whining at the couple. They were surprised. This powerful wolf was paying attention to them! The husband asked his wife, "You don't think that is Niki, do you?"

The lady said, "Niki couldn't have gotten that big. Maybe this wolf can just tell that we like wolves."

Lobo kept whining and wagging his tail with excitement. The young mother stared in disbelief. Finally she said, "Niki?" Lobo whined as if to say yes. He leaned against the cage for her to pet him. She bent over the rail and scratched his head through the wire. He licked her fingers. Then she knew in her heart that it was Niki.

Lobo finished greeting them. Then he went and laid down beside Missy. He licked Missy and looked back at the couple. It was like he was saying, "Hey, look what I found."

Just then Al Bristacoff walked by. The wife asked Al how the zoo got this male wolf.

Al answered, "It was about five years ago. The Humane Society in San Marino called. They asked if someone could come and tell them if they had found a wolf. As you can see, they had. He was about six months old when we brought him to the zoo. The wolf had on a red collar. He must have been someone's pet that got lost. Can you imagine someone keeping a wolf like that for a pet? They can become dangerous. Lobo's changed. He used to like everybody. But now just a few people can be sure that he won't attack them."

The couple thanked Al for talking with them. They stayed a few more minutes with their old friend. Lobo was playing with his pups. Missy was watching proudly.

"He's better off; it has worked out for the best, hasn't it?" asked the husband. "Our yard looks nice. And our new dog Skippy would never hurt anyone. We got to have Niki when he was a safe and loving puppy. We had him when it was best for us. The zoo got him when it was best for him. Doesn't he look happy?"

They left with their old questions finally answered. They knew things had worked out best for everyone.

The story of Niki always reminds me of my own life. Sometimes things don't work out the way I think they should. I become really upset. Yet, later I can look back at what has happened. And it has all turned out for the best.

The Bible says this in Romans 8:28: "We know that in everything God works for the good of those who love him." Isn't that a wonderful thing to know? God's taking care of you, even when you don't understand it. That's good enough for me. How about you?